3 3052 01208 6544

D0859676

When Molly and her brother Matthew wake up to find their yard blanketed in snow, they can hardly wait to get outside. Together they roll giant snowballs, placing them side by side. At day's end, Matthew and Molly haven't built ordinary snowmen. They've built *snowhorses!*

That night, while watching their snowhorses glow in the moonlight, Molly has an idea. When the moonlit horses spring magically to life, the ensuing adventure leaves Molly, Matthew, and readers breathless with excitement.

"McGeorge's writing is filled with action, excitement, and descriptive words that breathe life into the story, but Whyte's dynamic watercolor illustrations are what steal the show." — *Booklist*

"A very good story—thumbs up."
— *American Bookseller*

Constance W. McGeorge is a former teacher who lives in Ohio. A horse lover, she spends her leisure time riding her own horse, a seventeen-hand hunter. *Snow Riders* was inspired by her childhood memories of building snowhorses on winter days.

Mary Whyte, a graduate of Tyler Art School, is an accomplished artist best known for her watercolor paintings. She grew up in Ohio, and now lives in South Carolina with her husband and their golden retriever, Boomer.

For Smitty, with love
M. W.

For my mother
for helping Ginny and me
create our first snowhorses,
and for giving me my
first real horse
C. W. M.

Text © 1995 by Constance W. McGeorge.
Illustrations © 1995 by Mary Whyte. All rights reserved.
The illustrations in this book were rendered in watercolor. Typeset in Goudy Bold.
Book design by Laura Jane Coats. Printed in Hong Kong.
Library of Congress Cataloging-in-Publication Data
McGeorge, Constance W.
Snow Riders / by Constance W. McGeorge; illustrated by Mary Whyte.
32 p. 21.59 x 27.94 cm.
Summary: Matthew and his sister Molly build snowhorses that come to life
when they take a ride in the moonlight.
ISBN-10 0-8118-2464-0; ISBN-13 978-0-8118-2464-4
[1. Brothers and sisters—Fiction. 2. Snow—Fiction. 3. Horses—Fiction.]
I. Whyte, Mary, ill. II. Title.
PZ7.M478467Sn 1995 [E]—dc20 94-47214 CIP AC
Distributed in Canada by Raincoast Books
9050 Shaughnessy Street, Vancouver, British Columbia V6P 6E5
10 9 8 7 6 5 4 3
Chronicle Books
85 Second Street, San Francisco, California 94105
www.chroniclekids.com

SNOW RIDERS

by

CONSTANCE W. MCGEORGE

illustrated by

MARY WHYTE

chronicle books

San Francisco

Poudre River
Public Library
District

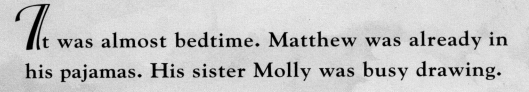

It was almost bedtime. Matthew was already in his pajamas. His sister Molly was busy drawing.

"It's snowing!" Matthew exclaimed.

"Maybe we'll get to stay home from school tomorrow," said Molly.

By morning, the neighborhood was buried in white. School was canceled. Molly and Matthew could hardly wait to go outside!

Molly rushed out into the yard and started rolling a snowball. Matthew helped her, and together they pushed the snowball through the deep snow. When it was finally big enough, they started to make another.

Molly and Matthew finished the second snowball, and then a third. But instead of stacking them one on top of the other, they placed them side by side, and then they made three more.

All day long they worked. They packed and pounded handfuls of snow over, under, and between the big snowballs. Finally, their creations were complete — with eyes and ears and flowing manes and tails!

But the sun was going down fast. Before they knew it, Molly and Matthew were called inside for supper.

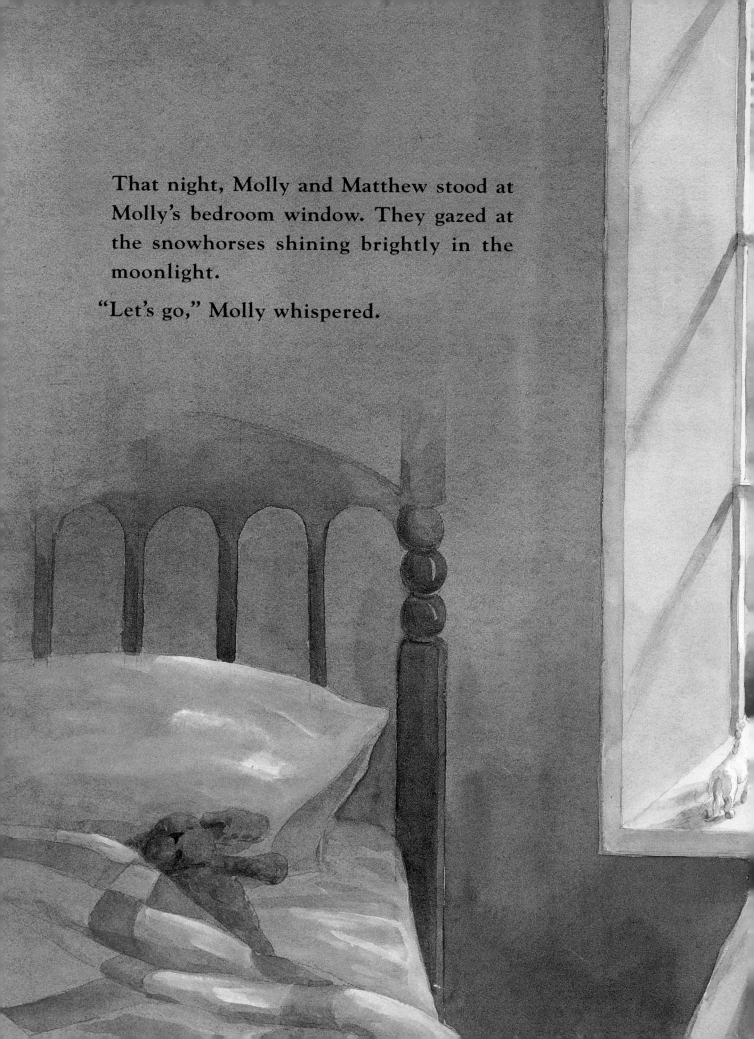

That night, Molly and Matthew stood at Molly's bedroom window. They gazed at the snowhorses shining brightly in the moonlight.

"Let's go," Molly whispered.

Crunch, crunch, they crept across the sparkling snow. Under the midnight moon, they climbed onto the cold, silent snowhorses. They held imaginary bridle reins and bounced up and down, pretending to ride.

Matthew kicked his heels into the side of his snowhorse. "Giddy-up!" he commanded.

Suddenly, the snowhorse swung its head around! It whinnied and flashed a bright shining eye.

Then Molly's horse shook its head and tail. Powerful long legs unfolded, and with a rumble, the giant horses heaved themselves upward.

The horses pranced in place and then cantered out of the yard. Molly and Matthew grabbed locks of mane and squeezed their legs tight against the horses' sides.

The horses splashed across an icy stream and through the woods into a wide open field.

Then the horses started to race! Ears back, necks flat, they charged into a full gallop, tearing across the field at lightning speed.

Molly and Matthew held on tight. Their faces tingled from the icy wind and the flying snow.

Suddenly, Molly saw something at the end of the field. It was a fence! Molly held her breath as her horse perked his ears and collected his stride. Then her horse tucked up his knees and jumped the fence clean.

"Lean forward," Molly shouted back at Matthew, "and don't look down!"

Matthew leaned forward, his face into the wind. His horse jumped high into the air and cleared the fence.

The horses galloped on. They crossed another open field and headed up a steep hill.

Finally, the horses slowed down to rest. Molly and Matthew looked out over the valley and up at the starry sky. They listened for a long time to the quiet of the night. The familiar sound of a train whistle drifted up the hill. "Is that the morning train?" asked Matthew.

The horses turned and started walking down the hill. The moon lit the way to Molly and Matthew's front yard. The horses were warm and steam rose from their backs. They stood very still, with their heads held high, as their riders slid off. Molly and Matthew lingered a moment, stroking and patting the horses. Then they turned away and slipped quietly back into the house.

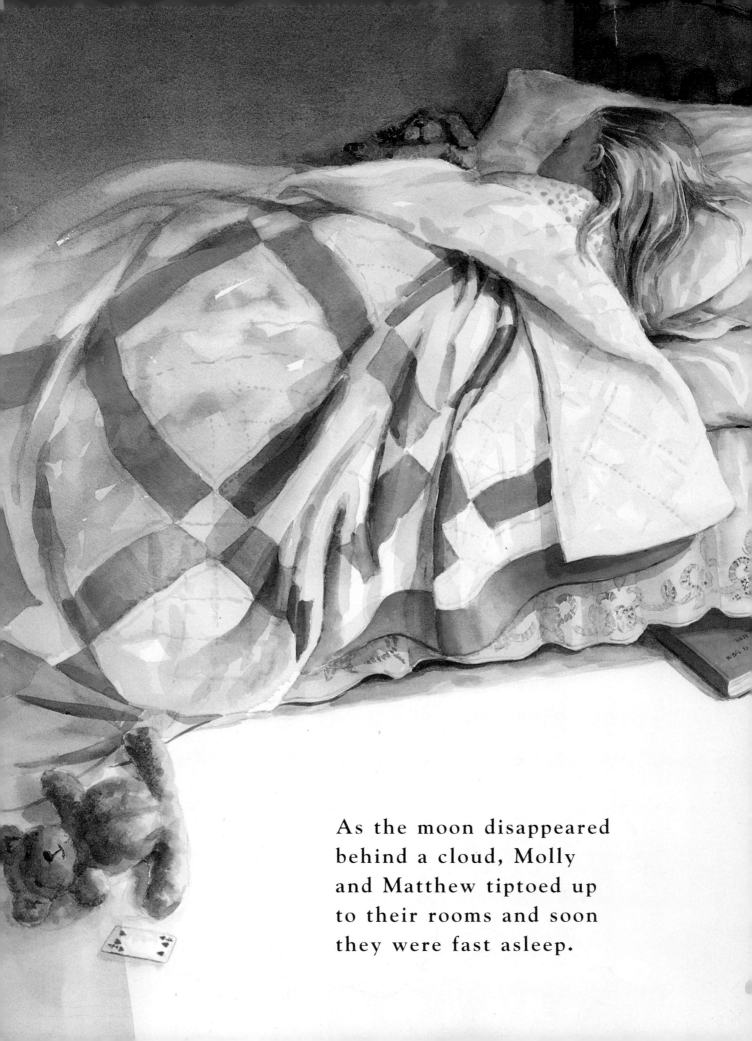

As the moon disappeared
behind a cloud, Molly
and Matthew tiptoed up
to their rooms and soon
they were fast asleep.

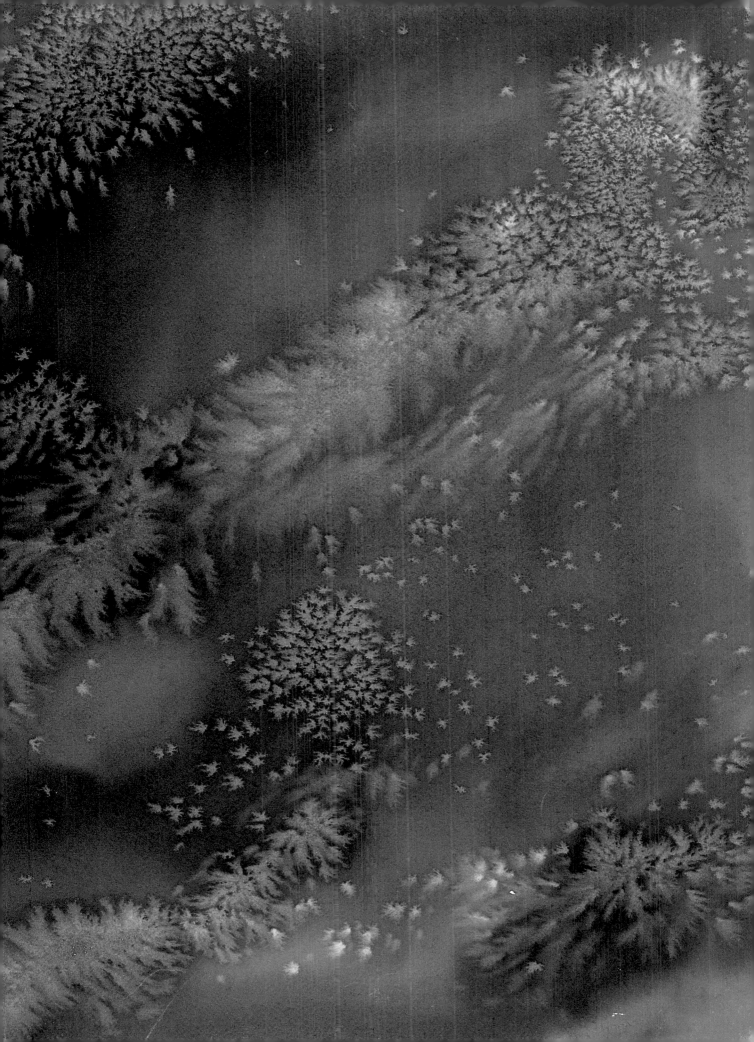

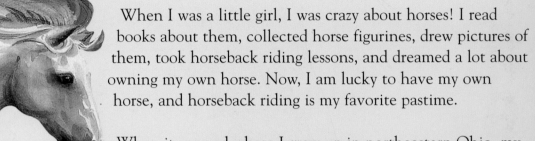
A NOTE FROM THE AUTHOR

When I was a little girl, I was crazy about horses! I read books about them, collected horse figurines, drew pictures of them, took horseback riding lessons, and dreamed a lot about owning my own horse. Now, I am lucky to have my own horse, and horseback riding is my favorite pastime.

When it snowed where I grew up in northeastern Ohio, my sister and I would build snowhorses instead of snowmen. So you see, I've drawn on my childhood dreams and activities to create a fantasy story I hope you find fun and exciting.

Take time to look at Mary Whyte's beautiful watercolor illustrations. They capture the wonder and beauty of winter, and remind me of the winter days of my childhood — waiting and watching for snow!

Connie McGeorge

A GUIDE TO USING THIS BOOK

Snow Riders can be used as a springboard for discussion about hobbies, seasons, dreams, and the power of imagination. As the book is read aloud, allow time for everyone to look closely at the illustrations. Children will enjoy pointing out when the snowhorses come alive as well as discussing the fun and excitement that the winter season holds!

DISCUSSION TOPICS

• In the first spread Molly is busy drawing. What is she drawing? Are there other signs in the picture that Molly likes horses? What are they?

• There are no calendars or clocks pictured in the story. How do you know what time of year it is? How do you know what time of day it is at different points in the story?

• Molly and Matthew make horses out of snow. What other things can be made out of snow? Have you ever made something out of snow?

• Some seasonal activities — like Molly and Matthew building snowhorses during the winter — become annual traditions. What is a tradition? What traditions does your family have each year? In what season does this story take place? What are seasons? Describe some special things that happen each season.

• Do you think the snowhorses really came alive or was it a dream?